D0688643

DATE DUE

FEB 2 2 '9	3		
MAR. 3 '92	3		
MAR. 10 '92	9		
	2		
JAN 5	2		
JAN 11	2		
JAN 2 9 1996			
APR 1 2 1996			

Series 606D

'WELL-LOVED TALES'

The Little Red Hen
and the grains of wheat

A LADYBIRD 'EASY READING' BOOK

retold by VERA SOUTHGATE M.A. B. Com,
with illustrations by ROBERT LUMLEY

Publishers: Ladybird Books Ltd . Loughborough
© Ladybird Books Ltd (formerly Wills & Hepworth Ltd) 1966
Printed in England

THE LITTLE RED HEN
and the grains of wheat

Once upon a time, there was
a little red hen who lived in a
farmyard.

7214 0084 1

One day the little red hen found some grains of wheat.

She took them to the other animals in the farmyard.

"Who will help me to plant these grains of wheat?" asked the little red hen.

" Not I,"

said the cat.

" Not I,"

said the rat.

" Not I,"

said the pig.

"Then I shall plant the grains myself," said the little red hen.

So she did.

Every day the little red hen went to the field to watch the grains of wheat growing.

They grew tall and strong.

One day, the little red hen saw that the wheat was ready to be cut.

So she went to the other animals in the farmyard.

"Who will help me to cut the wheat?" asked the little red hen.

"Not I,"
      said the cat.

"Not I,"
      said the rat.

"Not I,"
      said the pig.

"Then I shall cut the wheat myself," said the little red hen.

So she did.

"The wheat is now ready to be made into flour," said the little red hen to herself, as she set off for the farmyard.

"Who will help me to take the wheat to the mill, to be ground into flour?" asked the little red hen.

"Not I,"

said the cat.

"Not I,"

said the rat.

"Not I,"

said the pig.

"Then I shall take the wheat to the mill myself," said the little red hen.

So she did.

The little red hen took the wheat to the mill and the miller ground it into flour.

When the wheat had been ground into flour, the little red hen took it to the other animals in the farmyard.

"Who will help me to take this flour to the baker, to be made into bread?" asked the little red hen.

" Not I,"
said the cat.

" Not I,"
said the rat.

" Not I,"
said the pig.

"Then I shall take the flour to the baker myself," said the little red hen.

So she did.

The little red hen took the
flour to the baker and the baker
made it into bread.

When the bread was baked, the little red hen took it to the other animals in the farmyard.

"The bread is now ready to be eaten," said the little red hen. "Who will help me to eat the bread?"

"I will,"

said the cat.

"I will,"

said the rat.

"I will,"

said the pig.

"No, you will not," said the little red hen. "I shall eat it myself."

So she did.

Series 606D